Baby, Come Away

Victoria Adler

Pictures by

David Walker

Farrar Straus Giroux
New York

For Tessa and Julian, my heart's delight
—V.A.

For a very special friend, Mia Louise
—D.W.

Text copyright © 2011 by Victoria Adler
Pictures copyright © 2011 by David Walker
All rights reserved
Distributed in Canada by D&M Publishers, Inc.
Color separations by KHL Chroma Graphics
Printed in July 2011 in China by Macmillan Production (Asia) Ltd.,
Kwun Tong, Kowloon, Hong Kong (supplier code WKT)
Designed by Roberta Pressel
First edition, 2011
1 2 3 4 5 6 7 8 9 10

mackids.com

Library of Congress Cataloging-in-Publication Data
Adler, Victoria.
    Baby, come away / Victoria Adler ; pictures by David Walker.
      p.   cm.
    Summary: A bird, a cat, a dog, and a fish each imagines an
ideal day spent with a baby.
    ISBN: 978-0-374-30480-5
    [1. Stories in rhyme.   2. Babies—Fiction.   3. Animals—Fiction.]
I. Walker, David, 1965–   ill.   II. Title.

PZ8.3.A2328Bab 2011
[E]—dc22
                                                            2010036234

Baby,

come away.

Let's fly up high
To my nest
In the sky
Where the green leaves rustle
And the clouds drift by.

You'll rest

As a guest

In your Sunday best.

With a bird suit, feather cap, stockings on your legs,

You'll warm my eggs

And we'll have tea

In our tip-top tree.

A worm for you
And a worm for me.
Baby, take a bite!

We'll munch, munch, munch
To our hearts' delight!

Baby,

come away.

Let's play
In the barn
With a catnip mouse
And a ball of yarn.

We'll tangle and twist it
Till it's one big knot!

When it's hot
We'll sneak
To the creek
With pitter-patter feet

And float on a boat
In a milk-white sea.
With a dipper and a cup
We'll sip it up.

Milk for you
And milk for me,
Creamy and white.
We'll sip, sip, sip
To our hearts' delight.

Baby,

come away.

Let's run in the sun
Past the garden patch.

I'll throw you a twig
And we'll play catch
With a skip and a jump
And a tumble all around.

Let's romp and roll
In a puddle-filled hole,
Splish-splish splashing
With a bright new ball

Till down we fall
By the shade of a tree.

A bone for you
And a bone for me.
Baby, take a bite!
We'll chew, chew, chew
To our hearts' delight.

Baby,

come away.

Let's glide side by side
In the ocean wide.
We'll sink down deep
Where the mermaids sleep
And the cold crabs creep.

We'll dwell in a shell
Like a queen and a king.
The crabs will fiddle
And the clams will sing.

We'll dance in a ring

In the deep, deep sea

With a toe tap, finger snap, circle on the sand.

An octopus will take your hand.

A dance for you
And a dance for me.

Baby, hold tight!
We'll twirl, twirl, twirl
To our hearts' delight.

Baby in a tree,
Baby in the sea,
Baby running free,
At the end of the day
Come back to me.

I'll take you in my arms
And hold you tight
And rock, rock, rock you in the darkening light
Till the stars are shining and the moon is bright.

A kiss for you and a kiss for me.

Baby, good night.

Dream, dream, dream
To your heart's delight.